For the children of St Anne's School, Alderney

Text copyright © 1993 Elisabeth Beresford
Inside illustrations © 1993 James Mayhew
Cover illustrations © 2001 James Mayhew

First published in Great Britain in 1993
by Simon & Schuster Young Books
This edition published in 2001 by Hodder Children's Books

10 9 8 7 6 5 4 3 2 1

A Catalogue record for this book is available from the British Library

ISBN 0 340 79517 4

Printed by Wing King Tong, Hong Kong

Hodder Children's Books
A Division of Hodder Headline Limited
338 Euston Road, London NW1 3BH

ELISABETH BERESFORD

Lizzy's War

Illustrated by JAMES MAYHEW

Hodder
Children's
Books

a division of Hodder Headline Limited

Chapter One

Lizzy neither heard nor saw the bomb which hit her house. One moment it was just an ordinary Saturday afternoon and the next. . . . Lizzy was sitting in the living room with her mother and her headmistress, Miss Lock, who had come to lunch and Lizzy had hardly uttered a word. She wasn't saying much now, just sitting on the edge of the sofa wondering if she and her mother would be able to go to the cinema tonight. Lizzy loved the cinema; next to reading and swimming it was her most favourite thing in the world.

The big, heavy orange velvet curtains were
drawn across the windows although it was a
lovely summer's day. This was because the
air-raid warning had sounded a few minutes
ago which meant there might be some enemy
planes about and sometimes when the guns
down the road went off they were so loud
they broke the windows and glass went
everywhere. The curtains were supposed to
stop that happening. An air-raid shelter was
being built at the school, but it was only half
finished.

Lizzy's mother had just asked Miss Lock if
she would like another cup of coffee when the
most extraordinary thing happened.

One minute Lizzy was just sitting there and the next she was sitting on top of the tall bookcase on the other side of the room. There she was six feet above the carpet — which was now covered in glass and mud from the window boxes on what had been the balcony but was now bits of concrete mixed up with plaster from the ceiling. And the furniture was all over the place.

Everything got a bit muddled after that.
There was grey dust everywhere and some of
the front of the house was now lying in the
basement. The whole street was in a terrible

mess and an air-raid warden, who was also the local greengrocer, asked Lizzy if she'd look after some small children in the house opposite because their mother wasn't at home. So Lizzy sat on the dusty stairs with them while more men arrived and began trying to clear up.

Some time later Lizzy's mother – who also looked very dusty, which was most unlike her, came to collect her and they went to stay with Doctor Hemming who was an old friend. Everybody else talked a lot about what had happened, but Lizzy hardly spoke at all, although she quite enjoyed sleeping on cushions on the floor under the grand piano which had been turned into a kind of air-raid shelter. But Lizzy thought it was more like a mysterious cave.

As all Lizzy's toys and books had vanished Miss Lock very kindly gave her an encyclopedia with pictures.

Lizzy's mother made some telephone calls, packed up Lizzy's suitcase and said they were off to meet a new friend. They travelled on a small bus out into the country until they reached a village.

It was lucky they only had one small suitcase and a shopping basket between them because it was quite a long and dusty walk until they reached the end of a twisting lane, just before it became a cart track.

"This is it," said Lizzy's mother, sounding quite nervous for her. She was very small, hardly taller than Lizzy, but it seemed as if she had never been frightened of anything in her life. And she straightened Lizzy's blue beret right down over her eyes, and tugged at Lizzy's cotton dress. Then she pushed open a rickety garden gate and went up to the front door of a small house and rang the bell.

Bees buzzed, a black cat came out of a lavender bush and stalked past them. Swallows dipped and dived up and down the lane, but nobody answered the door.

"Oh dear," said Lizzy's mother even more nervously and she rang again. Nothing happened.

"I wonder," said a polite voice, "if you could be looking for *me*? I was in the orchard, you know, with Popeye."

A rather large old lady was looking at them
from round the side of the house. She had a
creased and crumpled face and she was
wearing a long cardigan with holes in it and a
long dress with the hem coming down.
Under one arm was a very fluffy Pekinese
dog with its tongue lolling out, and in her
other hand was a half eaten apple. She tried to
push it into her pocket, but it was too full and
it bounced out again. Lizzy picked it up and
politely handed it back. They looked at each
other. Lizzy's mother said in a faint voice,

"Miss Damps?"

"Well, yes. I'm so sorry, the front door
seems to be locked for some reason. So Lizzy
is coming to stay with me. That's a very
good idea. Don't you think so, Lizzy?"

They looked at each other in a considering
way and then Lizzy wiped her dusty hand on
her skirt and held it out. Miss Damps put
down Popeye and they shook hands. Lizzy
looked up from under her beret and spoke her
first proper words since the invisible bomb.

"Good morning, Miss Damps."

Chapter Two

Lizzy watched her mother get on the bus to be driven away – perhaps for ever? – and felt a bit wobbly.

"She'll be back next weekend," said Miss Damps. "Look what I found in my pocket. I can't think how it got there." And she produced a very old paper bag with two toffees in it. They were a bit melted, but once Lizzy had got one in her mouth and was shifting it from cheek to cheek there didn't seem to be any room left in her face for tears.

"I used to have a car," said Miss Damps.
"My nephew taught me to drive it. Well,
almost taught me to drive it. But They made
me put it away for the Duration. I'm not
quite certain what that means, something to
do with how long there's a war?" And she
looked hopefully at Lizzy. Lizzy shook her
head. She couldn't have answered if the King
had suddenly appeared out of the dusty hedge
and spoken to her.

Popeye snuffled along beside them and then decided to chase a rabbit and got caught in the hedge. Lizzy went in after him and Miss Damps pulled until he came free and sneezed violently.

"Don't know
what I'd do without
you, Lizzy," said Miss
Damps, whose cardigan
was now more full of holes than ever.
"Let's see what your mother's left us
for supper. She seems to be a very good cook."

Lizzy nodded. When they opened the ancient refrigerator they found food for the whole week with tickets on: 'Monday', 'Tuesday' . . . which explained why Lizzy's mother had been so busy over the weekend. It was just as well, as Miss Damps was *not* a very good cook. In fact she couldn't cook at all, although she had some very unusual ideas about it. At breakfast she looked at the pot of marmalade, which had become so thick that Lizzy's spoon bent when she tried to get some out.

"Soon deal with that," said Miss Damps and poured some boiling tea into it. It worked very well.

Lizzy, who had slept wonderfully after three helpings of vegetable pie, asked if she could go exploring.

"Go where you like," said Miss Damps, peering at a cookery book and sighing.

Lizzy went to open the front door. She had to pull it hard because it had stuck, so she got the encyclopedia and used it to prop the door open.

"Always thought it would come in useful," Lizzy said, sounding just like her mother and went off to explore with Popeye at her heels.

They got as far as the front garden and the garage. Popeye went and sniffed at the garage and barked.

"He always does that," Miss Damps said from round the side of the house. She had given up the cookery book and started gardening. She had taken off all her rings and they were now hanging from the currant bushes and sparkling in the sunshine. Lizzy thought they looked like magic raindrops.

Lizzy went and joined Popeye and they both sniffed. A very strange and powerful smell was coming through the cracks in the garage door.

Lizzy put her eye to one of them but it was too dark inside to see anything. Lizzy went and got Miss Damps and the three of them sniffed together.

"The car's been in there for a long time," said Miss Damps. "Perhaps it's gone off like cheese does. We'll have to open up. Lizzy, get the breadknife!"

They took it in turns to work on the lock and the breadknife got a funny bend in it, but suddenly the door creaked open and a truly dreadful smell came out. All three of them stepped back and sneezed.

"Lizzy, do be careful," said Miss Damps holding her nose. "Oh, I remember now, I put some apples on the roof netting to make cider . . ."

Bravely, Lizzy stepped into the smelly gloom, scowling dreadfully under her beret. A very unusual sight met her eyes. The apples had long since rotted away and had oozed through the netting and into Miss Damps' open-topped car. That was bad enough, but worse was to come, for floating in the sludge *inside* the car were some very dead rats.

"Dear me," said Miss Damps from behind a handkerchief. She and Lizzy looked at each other. "I think I'll get old Arthur from further down the lane to come and clear up. I don't suppose the car will go very well after this."

They shut the door and propped it with a stone from the rock garden.

"I think, perhaps," said Miss Damps, "that we won't tell your mother about this."

Lizzy grinned.

"No, Miss Damps."

They went off hand in hand with Popeye snuffling at their heels to find old Arthur from further down the lane.

Chapter Three

It was a beautiful morning and Lizzy was
sitting on the swing which was on one side of
what had once been a football pitch and was
now allotments. The swing was very old.
But Lizzy didn't mind. She really enjoyed it
and sometimes she went so high the whole
thing shuddered and groaned. There were
some other children playing on the far side of
the allotment and Lizzy was just rocking
gently and half listening to them when she
heard a plane flying very fast. Lizzy squinted
up at the brilliant blue sky and went on
rocking.

There was a very loud rat-a-tat-tat and in
the distance an air-raid siren sounded its
moaning call. Lizzy always half expected to
see some great dragon winging across the sky
when she heard that sound, but instead she
saw a small plane which was getting rapidly
larger.

"Coming down," Lizzy said
knowledgeably to herself. It was coming
down so fast it was making a screaming
sound.

Up above it she could see a white parachute
dangling its way down to earth, but it was
the plane that was really interesting . . . It
was turning round and round now and the
noise was amazing. The other children had
got down flat on the ground so Lizzy thought
she had better do the same although the plane
was spinning away from them now.

There was the most tremendous explosion
and bits of metal and pieces of trees went in
all directions and every bird in the district
went straight up into the sky. Lizzy was
fascinated, this would be something to tell
her mother at the weekend!

She jumped to her feet and watched the other children running up and down and picking up bits of wreckage and then sucking their fingers.

"Souvenirs," Lizzy thought to herself. "I wish I'd got one . . ."

And then she saw it, lying quite close to her, in among the vegetables – a chunky piece of grey metal about the size of a waste-paper basket.

The moment Lizzy picked it up she knew why the others had started licking their fingers. It was *hot*!

"Here you, blooming kids," shouted a man's voice, and over the far side Lizzy saw a man in an air-raid warden's uniform, blowing a whistle and running after the children, who took to their heels like greyhounds.

It was definitely time to go. Luckily Lizzy
had a handkerchief with her and she wrapped
it round the piece of metal and took to her
heels. Only just in time, because old Albert
from down the lane suddenly appeared
driving his rickety old van with a whole lot of
Home Guard men in the back. They were all
waving and shouting too. Lizzy vanished into
the little copse of trees.

"Well," said Miss Damps, "I wonder what it *is*?"

They surveyed the strange, almost bottle shaped object.

"Perhaps old Albert from down the lane might know. He's bringing in a chicken after dark." Miss Damps lowered her voice and closed one eye. Lizzy's mind was on her wonderful souvenir.

"It'd make a good doorstop," Lizzy said. The encyclopedia was getting a bit warped. Popeye sniffed at the metal bottle, barked and waddled off to sit and pant behind the sofa.

It made a first-rate doorstop and they were very proud of it, but neither Popeye nor the

cat would go near it. It was very odd and when Lizzy patted it Popeye barked like a mad thing and went racing off into the scrubby little orchard. He lay out there whining and the cat had vanished altogether.

"I don't understand it," said Miss Damps. "Now then Lizzy, I've done a swap with old Albert; a bucket of my apples for one of his chickens. That'll be a treat for your mother."

Lizzy nodded, her mouth watering. She couldn't remember the last time she'd eaten chicken.

After supper, when it was getting towards
dusk, they went and stood by the garden
gate. It was very quiet with bats swooping
over their heads. And then they heard the
squeak squeak of old Albert's bicycle as he
came up the the lane.

"Better put that light out, Miss Damps,"
he said. "We don't want no air-raid warden
sticking his nose into what doesn't concern
him. I'll just take the bird through. It's a good
'un and . . . WHAT'S THAT!"

His face had gone a funny colour and he was backed right up against the wall.

"Our new doorstop," said Miss Damps. "Lizzy found it after that plane came down this morning. Aren't you feeling well? Do you know which bit of the plane it might be?"

"I might . . ." his voice was hoarse, "just fill a bucket, *quick*!"

He was really behaving in a very strange way because the moment Miss Damps handed it to him he made her and Lizzy go into the kitchen and shut the door.

They heard him tip-toe as quietly as he could in his boots down the passage and then he gave a kind of gasp and there was a woosh of water.

"I do believe he's put our doorstop in the bucket," said Miss Damps, her eye to the keyhole, "and now he's taken it out into the garden and put it in the lane and . . ."

"Put that light out!" a voice shouted in the distance.

The front door shut with a thud and Albert's boots came noisily down the passage with Popeye and the cat at his heels.

He came into the kitchen and sat down heavily. Miss Damps went to the cupboard under the sink and got out a dusty bottle of beer. Old Albert took out the stopper and drank it straight down and then wiped his sleeve across his mouth.

"That doorstop of yours could've been an unexploded bomb. I'm not sure, but I've put it into the bucket to make it safe. Could've blown you all to smithereens!"

After he'd gone Lizzy and Miss Damps looked at each other and then at the rather dusty chicken.

"I don't think we'd better tell my mother about it," said Lizzy.

"No, Lizzy," said Miss Damps.

Chapter Four

"You know, Lizzy," said Miss Damps, "I've really enjoyed your staying here. But I daresay your mother may have found somewhere else for you both . . ."

Lizzy's heart seemed to go up and down at the same time. She was really looking forward to seeing her mother, but on the other hand she very much liked being here with Miss Damps. It was very difficult. They looked at each other and then away and Miss Damps started putting the apples into her cardigan pockets instead of the old tin bucket. It made Lizzy think of the first time they'd met.

The bus arrived in a cloud of dust. It was very full and everybody seemed to be carrying a lot of luggage and just as Lizzy was starting to get anxious her mother got off.

She had two enormous shopping bags and she and Lizzy both talked at once. Lizzy's mother kept saying how well she looked and Lizzy had forgotten how small her mother was. And how neat and tidy.

Miss Damps was waiting for them at the door (re-propped open with the encyclopedia) and there was a lot more talk and then Miss Damps opened the oven door to show off the chicken. Lizzy's mother looked a bit surprised to see it just sitting on a plate which was already starting to crack. And then in some mysterious way Lizzy's mother just took over the cooking and it was wonderful. Much later Lizzy listened to the sound of talking down below as she drifted off to sleep. She didn't know *what* she wanted; to stay here with Miss Damps or go back with her mother?

In the morning when Miss Damps was still upstairs Lizzy's mother said; "Lizzy dear, I'm very sorry, but you may have to stay here for a while, because I'm still staying with friends. But I'm sure I'll be able to find somewhere for both of us before too long. This marmalade's got an unusual taste . . . and of course I can come and see you once a fortnight."

"Ah," said Lizzy.

"It does worry me a little, you being here. Are you sure you're all right? I mean Miss Damps is a bit unusual. You certainly look very well, but are you happy?"

Lizzy nodded vigorously. She felt just like Popeye did when he suddenly went mad and rolled over and over and chased his own silky tail.

Her mother leant closer and said in a whisper, "I just wondered if Miss Damps was worried about money? She doesn't wear those beautiful rings any more. Perhaps she's had to sell them . . ."

Lizzy paused with her mouth open. A picture of sparkling currant bushes passed

before her eyes. What *would* her mother say if she knew about *that*! She might think Miss Damps was really, *really* unusual . . .

"Postman," said Lizzy, "I think . . ."

She darted out of the kitchen just as Miss Damps came down the stairs.

"Rings," whispered Lizzy and put her finger to her lips as she hurried down the passage. They were all still there, exactly as Miss Damps had left them when she did her gardening. Diamonds and blue and red and green stones all glittering in the sunlight and freshly cleaned by the dew. Lizzy wrapped them in her (almost) clean handkerchief and returned on tip-toe.

Miss Damps was sitting at the kitchen table with her hands in her pockets. Lizzy's mother was standing at the sink with her back to them.

"Sorry, it wasn't the postman," mumbled Lizzy. She passed across the handkerchief, they both blew out their cheeks and suddenly Lizzy began to smile in a way she hadn't done since the silent bomb.

"Good morning, Miss Damps," said Lizzy and sat down for a second breakfast.

h HODDER *Another title by Elisabeth Beresford from Hodder Children's Books . . .*

THE SEQUEL TO *LIZZY'S WAR*:

Lizzy Fights On
Illustrated by James Mayhew

"Wouldn't it be wonderful if Daddy did come home one day?"

Lizzy and her friend Miss Damps find lots to do in the country to help the war effort, like collecting scrap metal and saving precious clothing coupons. But Lizzy really misses her dad, who has gone away to fight. Then one day, her mum suddenly discovers that she might know where he is . . .

The King in the Forest
Written by Michael Morpurgo
Illustrated by Tony Kerins

Something was moving at the edge of the forest, something white and small.

As a boy, Tod saves the small white fawn from certain death at the hands of the King's huntsmen. Tod and the fawn grow up together, until the fawn becomes a fine, white stag, and leaves, to become the "King in the Forest". But no kingdom can have *two* kings. Will Tod's devotion to his boyhood friend prove strong enough to save his life once more?

The Shoemaker's Boy
Written by Joan Aiken
Illustrated by Alan Marks

"I have come to ask a favour of you . . ."

It is a night for visitors for Jem, the shoemaker's boy, working alone in his father's famous shop. First, three strange green children ask him for a set of silver keys, which he knows nothing about. Then a black knight comes requesting a fine pair of boots – and also asks for keys. But the third visitor proves to be the strangest – and most magical – of them all . . .